W9-BNR-172

THE NIGHT HAS EARS

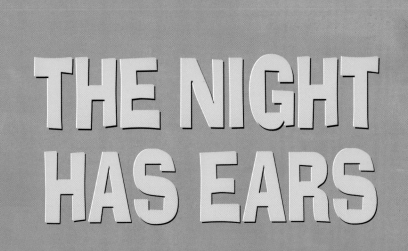

To Don, Sheri, and Don Jr. Pannell

and

In Loving Memory of my sister, Emerald

CONEJO VALLEY UNIFIED
SCHOOL DISTRICT
Thousand Oaks Library

THE NIGHT HAS EARS

African Proverbs

selected and illustrated by ASHLEY BRYAN

A Jean Karl Book

Atheneum Books for Young Readers

Atheneum Books for Young Readers
An imprint of Simon & Schuster Children's Publishing Division
1230 Avenue of the Americas
New York, New York 10020

Illustrations copyright © 1999 by Ashley Bryan

All rights reserved including the right of reproduction
in whole or in part in any form.

Book design by Michael Nelson

The text of this book is set in Breughel.
The illustrations are rendered in tempera and gouache.

Manufactured in China
10 9 8 7 6 5 4

Library of Congress Cataloging-in-Publication Data
Bryan, Ashley.
The night has ears : African proverbs / selected and illustrated by Ashley Bryan.
p.   cm.
"A Jean Karl Book"
Summary: A collection of twenty-six proverbs, some serious and some
humorous, from a variety of African tribes.
ISBN 0-689-82427-0
I. Proverbs, African. [1. Proverbs, African.] I. Bryan, Ashley.
PN6519.A6N54   1999   398.9'096—dc21
98-48772

INTRODUCTION

I grew up in a household of proverbs. My mother had a proverb ready for any situation, attitude, or event. As a child, I was soon able to anticipate and finish any proverb that she would start. I heard, "Well begun is half-done," "Don't count your chickens before they hatch," "Beauty is what beauty does," "Rome was not built in a day," "Practice makes perfect," "Never weary in doing good," and many more. You probably have heard some of them.

African proverbs have also become familiar to me through my research of African tales. In making this selection, I have chosen proverbs from a number of tribes and have indicated them with the text. But none of the proverbs are exclusive to the tribe named. Many occur in other tribes as well. That is no surprise, for proverbs dramatize experiences common to all. It is therefore likely that you will find among them equivalents to proverbs you already know.

Proverbs abound in the oral traditions and written literatures of all people. They may be an accumulative list, as in the Biblical book of Proverbs, or exist as the collective sayings of any specific group. In their apt summarizations, they give insights into the culture and customs of a people.

Proverbs may also inspire stories in which the plot is developed to illustrate the meaning of the proverb. Such stories often conclude with the proverb, as in Aesop's and LaFontaine's fables.

I have selected some proverbs that are serious and some that are humorous. In all cases they provoke thought. Proverbs seek to raise meaning out of our daily experiences. Ponder them and search for as many meanings as they may hold for you. Have fun!

If you cannot dance, you will say,
"The drumming is poor."

-Ashanti

A man with a cough cannot conceal himself.

-Yoruba

However long the night, the dawn will break.

-Hausa

The frog enjoys itself in the water, but not in hot water.

-Wolof

Any old pole will stop up a hole in the fence.

–Ba-ila

When you see clouds gathering, prepare
to catch rainwater.

–Gola

The house of the loud talker leaks.

-Zulu

As a crab walks, so walk its children.

-Kpelle

Patching makes a garment last long.

-Yoruba

A log may lie in the water for ten years,
but it will never become a crocodile.

-Songhai

BERKELEY UNIFIED
SCHOOL DISTRICT
Thousand Oaks Library

When a drummer beats his drum,
people far and near enjoy it.
-Gola

Never try to catch a black cat at night.
-Krahn

Treat your guest as a guest for two days;
on the third day, give him a hoe.

-Swahili

If the people of the town and village are all happy,
look for the chief.

-Krahn

The more a song is heard, the more it is appreciated.

-Zulu

A frisky child knocks his face against the rocks.

-Kpelle

If stars were loaves, many people would sleep out.

-Wolof

One cannot borrow a man's mouth
and eat onions for him.

–Fulani

The goat is not big in a cow town.

-Vai

Do not try to fight a lion if you are not one yourself.
-Swahili

You may grow taller, but no taller than your head.

–Bassa

There is no one-way friendship.

–Maasai

The cook does not have to be a beautiful woman.

-Shona

Take the drowning child from the water
before scolding it.

–Grebo

No one tests the depth of the river with both feet.
-Krahn

No one knows the story of tomorrow's dawn.
                                        –Ashanti